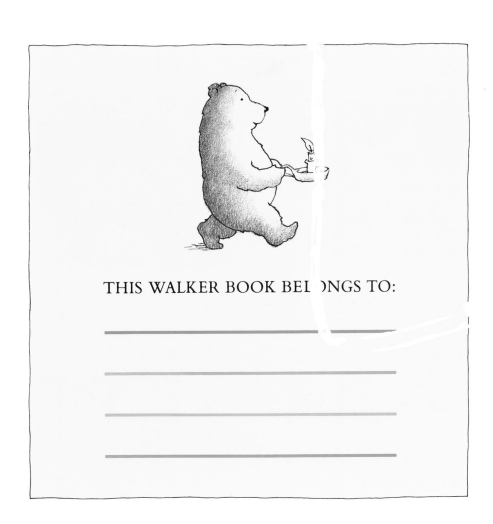

THIS WALKER BOOK BELONGS TO:

_____

_____

_____

_____

For Gemma

First published 1988 by Walker Books Ltd
87 Vauxhall Walk, London SE11 5HJ

This edition published 1990
Reprinted 1991 (twice)

© 1988 Chris Riddell

Printed in Hong Kong by
Sheck Wah Tong Printing Press Ltd

British Library Cataloguing in Publication Data
Riddell, Chris
The trouble with elephants.
I. Title
823'.914 [J]   PZ7
ISBN 0-7445-1309-X

THE
TROUBLE WITH
ELEPHANTS

Written and illustrated by
CHRIS RIDDELL

WALKER BOOKS
LONDON

The trouble with elephants is . . .

they spill the bath water
when they get in . . .

and they leave a pink elephant
ring when they get out.

They take all the bedclothes and they snore elephant snores which rattle the window panes.

The only way to wake a sleeping elephant is to shout "Mouse!" in its ear.

Then it will slide down the
bannisters to breakfast.

Elephants travel four in a car – two in the front and two in the back.

You can always tell when an elephant is visiting because there'll be a car outside with three elephants in it.

Sometimes elephants ride bicycles . . .

but not very often.

The trouble with elephants is that on elephant picnics they eat all the buns before you've finished your first one.

Elephants drink their lemonade through their trunks, and if you're not looking, they drink yours too.

On elephant picnics they play games
like leap-elephant and skipping,
which they're good at.

And sometimes they play hide and seek, which they're not very good at.

The trouble with elephants is . . .

well, there are all sorts of troubles . . .

all sorts of troubles . . .

but the real trouble is . . .

you can't help but love them.

MORE WALKER PAPERBACKS
For You to Enjoy

BEN AND THE BEAR
by Chris Riddell

There's lots of fun and jollity
When Ben invites the bear to tea!

ISBN 0-7445-1066-X   £2.99

THE FIBBS
by Chris Riddell

The Fibb family's tall stories are as funny as they are amazing.

ISBN 0-7445-1390-1   £2.99

CAN'T YOU SLEEP, LITTLE BEAR?
by Martin Waddell/Barbara Firth

Winner of the 1988 Smarties Book Prize and
the 1988 Kate Greenaway Medal.

"The most perfect children's book ever written or illustrated…
It evaporates and dispels all fear of the dark." *Molly Keane The Sunday Times*

ISBN 0-7445-1316-2   £3.99

**Walker Paperbacks are available from most booksellers, or by post from
Walker Books Ltd, PO Box 11, Falmouth, Cornwall TR10 9EN.**

To order, send:
Title, author, ISBN number and price for each book ordered
Your full name and address
Cheque or postal order for the total amount, plus postage and packing:

UK, BFPO and Eire – 50p for first book, plus 10p for
each additional book to a maximum charge of £2.00.
Overseas Customers – £1.25 for first book,
plus 25p per copy for each additional book.
Prices are correct at time of going to press, but are subject to change without notice.